Rhubarb

Written by: Stephen Cosgrove
Illustrated by: Robin James

A Serendipity™ Book

PRICE STERN SLOAN
Los Angeles

ISBN: 0-8431-2300-1

21 20 19 18 17 16

Dedicated to a delightful friend who is called many things: Rhubarb, Binkley, Beasley and Muffin, no matter that Ruby is really her name. My puppy, my friend in name, Ruby stays just the same.

Stephen

There was a farm called Rickity-Tickity in the land of Serendipity surrounded by fences of white weathered wood that wove through the meadows and fields. This farm was filled with simple animals that lived a simple life.

There lived on the Rickity-Tickity Farm all the creatures you would normally find on a farm. There were ducks and chickens and rabbits and cows, sheep and kittens and a mother pig, called a sow. They grunted, cackled, mooed and meowed as they lived their lives as nature allowed.

There also lived at Rickity-Tickity, a delightfully fuzzy little puppy. She was cute. She was cuddly. She was all those things that make you smile when you think of words like fluffy or friendly or furry. Most of all, she was just a tiny tail-wagging puppy who would just as soon lick you on the nose as say, "Good Morning."

Her name was Rhubarb, but all of her friends called her Ruby, for she shined like a sparkling jewel.

Ruby loved to play in and about the Rickity-Tickity Farm with all the creatures that lived there. The bunnies, the chickens and the sheep all loved to play with Ruby when she wasn't asleep.

The ducks that lived in the pond behind the barn loved to play with Ruby too. They would make up all sorts of silly duck games and flap their wings and chase her around and around.

Ruby would chase or be chased, no one could tell which for sure, until she would fall in a panting, laughing heap, watching as a frilly feather floated by in the air, coming to rest on the tip of her nose.

When she wasn't with the ducks, she could be found running about in the meadow with the sheep. Together they would run through fields of purpled clover. They would play tag and whoever was "it" would chase the others until with any luck he or she was able to lick another on the nose. (Oh yuck!)

Ruby loved this and would bound about the meadow jumping bits of clover that were bigger than she, just so she could lick some sheep upon the nose and say, "Tag! You're it!"

Ruby would even play with the pigs in the pen. Pigs play in a funny way, running about in the mud, rooting their noses like plows in a furrow, looking for secrets that surely were buried there. But Ruby would join right in just the same, searching and searching for she knew not what, until she was covered with muck. What a muddy mutt!

When Ruby and the pigs were finally pooped they would flop down in a patch of sunlight and let the sun bake their muddy bodies clean. Three little, pudgy pigs and a fluffy little puppy called Ruby.

Now, the problem, you see, was that all the animals that lived at Rickity-Tickity Farm loved to play with Ruby. She played with the ducks, the sheep and the pigs and when she wasn't playing she was resting so that she could play some more.

One day, as she was resting in the shade of a blooming lilac bush, the sheep and the ducks came looking to play with Ruby at the same time. The sheep were baaing and the ducks were quacking and Ruby woke up to find that she was being pulled this way and that by all of her friends.

To make matters worse, the pigs picked this very same time to fetch Ruby to go play in the mud. The normal peace and quiet of the farm was replaced by the squabbling sounds of the ducks quacking, the sheep baaing and the pigs oinking at the sun.

"She is ours!" quacked the ducks.

"No, she's not. She is ours!" baaed the sheep.

"You are both wrong!" squealed the pigs. "For Ruby belongs to us."

'Round and 'round they argued as to who was to play with Ruby and when.

Ruby continued to be pulled this way and that. The ducks pulled on her nose, the sheep pulled at her toes and the pigs yanked at her tail. Around the lilac bush they pushed and pulled their best fuzzy friend, until the dust got so thick that nobody could see.

All the animals finally stopped and when the dust settled, they discovered that Ruby was gone! They ran around the bush and looked and looked but nowhere could they find their furry, little friend. Still squabbling loudly, they raced about the barnyard looking for the gentle jewel, Ruby, but nowhere could she be found.

The lilac bush became a quiet place again as the bees buzzed about the blossoms. Deep inside and high upon the bush was a little dog hanging tightly to a branch looking very confused indeed. She didn't know what to do. She loved all her friends but they were loving her to distraction. She was nearly scared out of her wits and the bush, as a voice called out from the branches in a slow gentle drawl, "Watcha doing?"

Ruby spun her head and gripped the branch even tighter and there she saw, hanging upside down from a nearby branch, a possum.

"Well," she said as she scrambled up to where he hung, "my friends, the other barnyard animals, all want me to play and they're pulling me this way and that. I climbed the lilac bush to find some peace and quiet."

"Yuup," said the possum, "and quiet you might have found, except your friends are back." Sure enough, the barnyard critters had heard Ruby in the bush and had come racing from all points of the farm.

The ducks, the pigs and the sheep all raced around the tree calling for Ruby to come down and play.

"She is ours!" quacked the ducks.

"No, she's not. She is ours!" baaed the sheep.

"You are both wrong," squealed the pigs. "For Ruby belongs to us."

They argued and argued as to who was to play with Ruby and when.

"Ahem," interrupted the possum, "what are you speaking of?"

The farm animals were miffed at the interruption but answered, "Why, Ruby of course! She is our friend."

"Ahh," said the possum, "but a friend doesn't belong to anyone. Friendship is not something you own. Friendship is something you share. To have a friend, you must be a friend. There is no other way."

So, from that day forward, the animals that lived at Rickity-Tickity Farm shared their friendship and Ruby with all. She would play with the ducks, the sheep and the pigs and when she was tired she would share a cup of tea with the possum in a tree.

A FRIEND CANNOT BE OWNED
THAT IS PLAIN TO SEE
FRIENDSHIPS MUST BE SHARED,
JUST LIKE OUR FRIEND, RUBY

Serendipity™ Books

Created by Stephen Cosgrove and Robin James

Enjoy all the delightful books in the Serendipity™ Series:

BANGALEE	LITTLE MOUSE ON THE PRAIRIE
BUTTERMILK	MAUI-MAUI
BUTTERMILK BEAR	MAYNARD'S MERMAID
BUTTERWINGS	MEMILY
CATUNDRA	MING LING
CRABBY GABBY	MINIKIN
CREOLE	MISTY MORGAN
CRICKLE-CRACK	MORGAN AND ME
DRAGOLIN	MORGAN AND YEW
THE DREAM TREE	MORGAN MINE
FANNY	MORGAN MORNING
FEATHER FIN	THE MUFFIN MUNCHER
FLUTTERBY	MUMKIN
FLUTTERBY FLY	NAPOLEON'S RAINBOW
FRAZZLE	NITTER PITTER
GABBY	PERSNICKITY
GLITTERBY BABY	PISH POSH
THE GNOME FROM NOME	POPPYSEED
GRAMPA-LOP	RHUBARB
THE GRUMPLING	RAZ-MA-TAZ
HUCKLEBUG	SADIE
JALOPY	SASSAFRAS
JINGLE BEAR	SERENDIPITY
KARTUSCH	SNIFFLES
KIYOMI	SQUABBLES
LADY ROSE	SQUEAKERS
LEO THE LOP	TICKLE'S TALE
LEO THE LOP TAIL TWO	TRAPPER
LEO THE LOP TAIL THREE	WHEEDLE ON THE NEEDLE
ZIPPITY ZOOM	

The above books, and many others, can be bought wherever books
are sold, or may be ordered directly from the publisher.
Call toll-free: (800) 631-8571
PRICE STERN SLOAN
Customer Service Department
390 Murray Hill Parkway, East Rutherford, NJ 07073